BEACH BULLY

BY JAKE MADDOX

TEXT BY ERIC STEVENS

ILLUSTRATED BY ABURTOV

STONE ARCH BOOKS
a capstone imprint

Jake Maddox books are published by Stone Arch Books,
A Capstone Imprint
1710 Roe Crest Drive
North Mankato, Minnesota 56003
www.capstonepub.com

Library of Congress Cataloging-in-Publication Data
Maddox, Jake.
  Beach bully / by Jake Maddox ; text by Eric Stevens ; illustrated by Jesus
Aburto.
      p. cm. -- (Jake Maddox sports stories)
  Summary: Isaac and his parents have just moved into a house by the
ocean, and he is willing to try surfboarding, but there is a bully among the
local boys on the beach who seems determined to drive him away.
   ISBN 978-1-4342-5973-8 (library binding) -- ISBN 978-1-4342-6206-6 (pbk.)
1. Surfing--Juvenile fiction. 2. Bullying--Juvenile fiction. 3. Moving,
Household--Juvenile fiction. [1. Surfing--Fiction. 2. Bullies--Fiction. 3.
Moving, Household--Fiction.] I. Stevens, Eric, 1974- II. Aburto, Jesus, ill. III.
Title. IV. Series: Maddox, Jake. Impact books. Jake Maddox sports story.
  PZ7.M25643Bec 2013
  813.6--dc23

                         2012049367

Art Director: Bob Lentz
Graphic Designer: Veronica Scott
Production Specialist: Laura Manthe

Printed in the United States of America in
North Mankato, Minnesota.
082014   008432R

TABLE OF CONTENTS

CHAPTER 1

FROM SNOW TO SAND

"It looks small," Isaac Davis complained as his family's car pulled up in front of a little red house.

"It doesn't need to be big," his dad replied. "It's just the three of us. We don't need that much space."

"And it's cute!" his mom added. "The neighborhood is great, and the best part is we're only a block and half from the beach."

"The ocean, Isaac," his dad said. "Just think about it! You're steps from the ocean!"

Dad took a deep breath of the salty ocean breeze through the car's open window. "Ahh! I've missed it so much," he said.

Isaac rolled his eyes and grabbed his duffel off the seat next to him. He climbed out of the car and stood staring at his new home.

It was tiny, probably less than half the size of the house they'd lived in up north. Their old home had been built into the side of a mountain and was surrounded by tall pine trees. The old house had three fireplaces and a screening room in the basement for watching movies. Best of all, it had direct access to one of the best downhill ski and snowboard trails in the state.

Snowboarding here? Isaac thought. *It's never going to happen.*

Isaac shouldered his duffel and looked back at his snowboard, still strapped to the roof of Dad's car.

I'll never use it again, he thought. *Might as well leave it there.*

CHAPTER 2

A NEW HOME

Isaac sat on the front porch of the new house and looked around the yard. Or what there was of it anyway.

Unlike his old house, which had been surrounded by open space, the new house sat right on the street. There was no front yard to play in — just a tiny porch and the sidewalk. Mom had set up a few potted plants in front of the window, but they didn't make the house feel more like home.

Down the street, Isaac could see the top of a little sand dune on the far side of a narrow boardwalk. He could hear seagulls cawing as they circled overhead. Barges and steamships sounded horns and bells as they sailed into the harbor.

Above all the other noises, Isaac could hear voices shouting and laughing. They sounded like boys his age.

"Mom!" Isaac called through the open front window. "I'm going to walk down to the beach."

"Don't be gone too long," his mom called back. "The moving truck will be here soon. I'm going to need your help with the unloading and unpacking."

"Yeah, yeah," Isaac muttered as he stood up and headed for the beach.

Isaac strolled down the street. The rest of their new block was filled with rows of tiny houses. They were all brightly colored and crammed tightly together like books on a bookshelf. Some were red, others were bright blue or yellow.

There were a few houses painted a dismal deep gray, or a soft slate gray. The colors reminded Isaac of the sky over the mountain back home right before a winter storm rolled in.

Back home, Isaac thought miserably. *Not home anymore.*

Isaac walked across the boardwalk and stood on the far edge, staring down at the water below. From there, he could see north to where the harbor opened up into the Pacific Ocean. That's where the voices had come from.

Isaac shielded his eyes. He could see the boys he'd heard from his porch. They were walking toward the real beach, where ten-foot high waves crashed onto the sand. On their heads and under their arms, the boys toted boards with fins. Not snowboards, of course — surfboards.

CHAPTER 3

HITTING THE BEACH

Isaac took a seat at the top of the dune and watched as the boys got ready to surf. There were about ten boys his age down there. They all wore long board shorts in bright colors and patterns.

Most of the boys sat on the sand close to the water, talking and goofing around. But every few minutes, a small group would paddle out into the ocean and try to catch a wave.

The tallest boy in the group was obviously the best surfer. Even though all the other boys took breaks, he was in the water anytime a group paddled out to wait for a good wave.

Isaac watched as the tall boy lay flat on his board and paddled out farther than the others. When a couple of boys grabbed a wave to ride to the beach, he waited for a bigger one. Finally the perfect wave appeared, and the boy started paddling forward.

Isaac knew snowboarding. If the wave had been a downhill run on the mountain back home, he'd have known how to judge if was a tough and exciting ride, or an easy boring one. But he knew nothing about surfing. To Isaac, all the waves looked the same — huge and terrifying.

This boy wasn't scared, though. The wave swelled up over his head, threatening to crash down on him at any moment as he raced toward the sand.

The boy surfed up the underbelly of the wave, then zipped back toward the ocean floor as the water curled over his head. The foamy crest of the wave reminded Isaac of the snow sliding off the roof of his old home.

Then the curl of the wave started to tighten, and the tall boy on the board had to duck. But he still managed to stay on his feet, crouching low and zipping up and down the wave.

Then, just before the wave collapsed on him, the boy pointed the nose of his board toward the beach and coasted in.

His friends cheered and clapped as the boy hit the beach. He took it in with a smile. Then he spotted Isaac sitting at the top of the dune.

The boy pointed at him, and the others looked up too. The group turned and started walking up the dune toward him. Isaac got to his feet.

"What's up?" said the tall boy.

"Nothing," Isaac replied. He felt out of place here. Back home, he would have fit in just fine. But here at the beach, with everyone else in shorts and bathing suits, it was weird to be wearing jeans and a black T-shirt.

"What are you doing here? You're not a local," one of the other boys said, scowling at Isaac.

"I am now," Isaac said. "My family and I just moved in up the boardwalk. I'm Isaac."

A third boy with shaggy red hair and freckles grinned at him. "I'm Steve," he said. He pointed at the tall boy. "And the show-off over there is Jackson. Where did you move from?"

"Up north," Isaac started to say. "I'm from —"

"Canada?" Jackson interrupted sarcastically.

The other boys all started cracking up.

"No," Isaac said, but he felt his face turning red.

"Because you sound like you're from Canada," Jackson said. "Do you know how funny you sound when you talk?"

Isaac shrugged. "I didn't notice," he said. He hesitated for a moment. "Well, I have to help my parents finish unloading the moving truck. I should probably head home."

"Home?" Jackson repeated with a laugh. "I can hardly understand your accent. How do you say it?"

"Home?" Isaac repeated. He didn't get what was so funny. It sounded normal to him.

But the other guys laughed and laughed. Finally Isaac just turned around and walked off.

"Can't you take a joke, new kid?" Jackson shouted after him. "Relax, dude. We'll let you know when we start a hockey team, eh?"

As he reached the boardwalk, Isaac could still hear the boys laughing and copying his accent. The sound of their voices carried a little too well on the water.

CHAPTER 4

TO NEW BEGINNINGS

By the time the moving van was unloaded, Isaac and his parents were exhausted and sweaty. Dad checked online and found a taco place near their house that would deliver.

Most of their stuff was still in boxes or pieces, so the family sat cross-legged on a blanket on the floor to eat dinner.

Dad raised his drink and made a toast. "To new beginnings," he said.

He and Mom clinked their cans together happily, but Isaac just stared down at his half-eaten taco. It was filled with weird stuff like fish and cabbage. Back home, it would have been filled with ground beef and grated cheese.

One more thing I have to get used to, Isaac thought.

"Is something wrong, Isaac?" Mom said. "You look upset."

"What is it, kid?" Dad said.

Isaac picked up his can of pop and stared at the light reflecting off its top. "I want to get a surfboard," he said.

Dad raised his eyebrows, and Mom looked at him with a confused smile.

"A surfboard, huh?" Dad said.

"Well, I can't snowboard here," Isaac said.

"That's not true," Dad said. "There are plenty of mountains within an hour of here."

"Come on, Dad," Isaac said. "Those aren't mountains."

Mom laughed. "All right," she said. "So you want to try surfing. It's the thing to do around here. Why not?"

Dad looked at her and frowned. "Just like that?" he said. "You want to just give him a free surfboard?"

Mom put a hand on Isaac's shoulder and looked at Dad. "This move has been hard on Isaac," she said. "I think we should at least give him this. Maybe it'll help him make some new friends."

Dad sighed and smiled. "You're right," he said. "Okay, surfboard it is. You'll be riding those waves in no time, Isaac."

Isaac laughed. "I hope you're right," he said.

Dad held up his can of pop again. "To new beginnings," he said, "and new boards." And this time, Isaac clinked his can too.

CHAPTER 5

UNWELCOME

First thing the next morning, Isaac convinced his parents to buy him some board shorts. It was pretty clear he couldn't surf in his jeans or snowboard gear. They headed to a local surf shop nearby and bought the gear he'd need.

After he promised to help with unpacking later, Isaac picked out a blue wetsuit. Then he grabbed his new board and headed down to the beach.

The other boys were already there, in the same spot as the day before. When Steve spotted Isaac, he elbowed the boy closest to him and muttered something under his breath. They both turned to stare at Isaac.

Isaac couldn't hear what they were saying, but he could tell from their faces that they weren't happy to see him. He kept walking along the beach until he reached the lifeguard tower. There, he dropped his towel, changed his shoes, and walked toward the water with his board under his arm.

He could feel the group of local boys watching him. He did his best to copy what he'd seen them do the day before. He walked out into the water, put his new surfboard in front of him, and climbed on, lying down on his belly.

The moment he did, though, he slid off the back of the board and straight into the water. He came up coughing water and feeling embarrassed. He heard laughter from down the beach.

Isaac gritted his teeth and climbed back onto the board — or at least he tried to. No matter what he did, he slipped back off the board and fell into the water.

"Hey, kid," the lifeguard called from his tall chair. "You got any wax on that board at all, or what?"

The local boys down the beach went crazy with laughter.

Isaac walked awkwardly out of the water, carrying his board in both hands. He hefted the board as calmly as he could. He started to walk past the local boys.

Jackson wasn't letting it go, though. "Hey," he called out, jogging up from the surf toward the top of the dunes. "Wait a second."

"What?" Isaac said. He stopped walking but didn't look up at Jackson.

"Where are you from?" Jackson asked quietly. It was just the two of them this time, and Jackson didn't smile.

"Big Sky," Isaac muttered. "It's in Montana."

"I figured," Jackson said. "You ski up there?"

"Snowboard," Isaac said.

Jackson shook his head. "And you figured you could pick up surfing just like that, huh?" he snapped.

Isaac shrugged.

"Well, let me clue you in on something, clueless," Jackson said. He leaned down a little, his face only inches from Isaac's. "This is my beach. And I don't want some Canadian wannabe who can't even wax his own surfboard hanging around and looking like a dork. Got it?"

Isaac stared down at his feet. He realized he'd forgotten his towel and sandals in his rush to get out of there.

"I'm talking to you," Jackson said. "Got it?"

Isaac didn't answer. He didn't even nod.

Jackson reached out and shoved Isaac's shoulders with both hands, knocking him backward. Isaac struggled to stand, and the tail of his board dropped to the sand.

"Now take off, okay?" Jackson said. "And don't come back. Remember what I said. My beach."

Jackson strolled back toward the water, where his friends stood waiting for him with their boards. They'd all seen the whole thing.

Isaac dropped his board onto the dune and went back to collect his towel and sandals. He didn't want to face the other kids, but he knew he couldn't just leave his things lying there.

Then I'd have to explain why I left them, he thought.

When he reached the lifeguard tower, Isaac looked up at the lifeguard. "You could have helped me, you know," Isaac said with a scowl.

The lifeguard, who looked like he was probably still in high school, looked down from his giant chair. "Seriously?" he said. "Toughen up, bro, or you'll never make it on these beaches."

Fine, Isaac thought as he grabbed his things and hurried back to pick up his board. *Then that's what I'll do.*

CHAPTER 6

BEACH BULLY STRIKES AGAIN

That night, Isaac and his dad headed back to the surf shop for a wax kit. Then they checked the Internet for tips on how to wax a board.

"So first we apply the basecoat," Dad said, squinting at the screen of the laptop computer through his reading glasses. "That'll make it bumpy."

"So I won't slide off of it every five seconds," Isaac added.

They headed out to the back deck. They set Isaac's board on the deck, with its fin hanging off the edge, and started rubbing the wax on.

It was hard work. The basecoat wax, which was meant to last for at least a year, took lots of strength to put on. By the time the coat was bumpy enough that Isaac's feet could get a grip, it was time to eat dinner.

"Come on in, you two," Mom called out the back door to Isaac and Dad. "I've used the new kitchen and boiled some spaghetti. We might as well use the dining room table, too."

"We'll do the topcoat before you go to bed," Dad said, putting his arm around Isaac's shoulders.

"Okay," Isaac agreed as they headed inside.

* * *

The next morning, Isaac was up with the sun. He wanted to get to the beach and try out his freshly waxed board. More importantly, he wanted to get there before Jackson and his friends showed up.

Dad had kept his word the night before, and they'd put the topcoat on the surfboard after dinner. The sticky topcoat, which helped a surfer stay on his feet, had been much easier to apply than the tough basecoat.

As Isaac walked along the boardwalk toward the beach, he could feel the sticky wax against his side. The smell of coconut filled the air.

Isaac smiled as he caught sight of the empty beach beyond the harbor. The local boys weren't there yet.

I can get out on the water and practice without them watching, Isaac thought with relief. *Maybe I won't look like a dope this time.*

Isaac hung his towel from the bottom rung of the lifeguard's ladder. The chair was empty this morning.

I guess the lifeguard isn't even up this early, Isaac thought as he kicked off his sandals and headed for the water.

This time, Isaac had no trouble getting onto the board and staying on his stomach. He paddled through the waves near the sand, though they tried to push him back. It was hard work to get out far enough that standing up would seem worth the trouble.

Isaac decided to try a small wave first —
one that wouldn't curl up over his head and
crash him into the sand face-first.

He faced toward the beach like he'd
seen the other boys do and turned his head
to look for waves approaching behind
him. When a small hump came toward
him, Isaac startled paddling and pushed
himself onto his knees, and then to his feet.
Somehow, it worked. He was standing.

Isaac grinned and struggled to keep his
balance as the surfboard rolled along the
gentle wave toward the sand. But staying
on his feet was harder than he expected.

After just a couple of seconds, the board
shot up in front of him, and Isaac tumbled
backward. His arms waved in crazy circles,
and he landed hard on his back in a foot of
salty surf.

Isaac sat up in the shallow water and coughed. He rubbed his eyes, which burned with the salt and grit of the ocean. When he opened them, he saw a figure running across the beach toward him. He squinted and realized that it was the lifeguard, in his red and white shorts.

"You okay, newbie?" the lifeguard called to him.

Isaac nodded and tried to say "Yeah," but ended up coughing some more.

The lifeguard shook his head. "You really shouldn't be out here so early," the lifeguard said. He turned and headed back for his chair. "If you'd hit your head, you could've drowned."

"Sorry," Isaac said. He headed for the sand, dragging his surfboard behind him.

"Don't be sorry," the lifeguard said. "Just don't be stupid. If there's no lifeguard on duty, don't surf — especially if you don't even know how."

The lifeguard pulled out his phone and started poking at it. A moment later he was chatting away.

"Hey, Canada!" a voice suddenly yelled from up the beach.

Isaac groaned. Glancing up, he saw Jackson and his whole crew stomping along the sand from the harbor, right toward Isaac.

"My name isn't Canada. It's Isaac," Isaac said. He crossed his arms across his bare chest, suddenly very aware of how pale his skin looked compared to the tans of the local surfer boys.

"I don't care what your name is," Jackson said. He came to a stop right in front of Isaac. "You're on my beach."

"I am not," Isaac said.

"Didn't we go over this yesterday?" Jackson said, glancing over at his friends. "Because I thought we did."

Isaac shook his head. "Your beach is over there," he said. He pointed over Jackson's shoulder. "That's where you guys were all surfing yesterday."

"Ah," Jackson said with a grin. "I see. You're still confused. When I said 'my beach' I meant the entire beach. All the way from the Mexican border up to your home country of Canada. Get it?"

Isaac looked at his feet. "That's not fair," he said quietly.

"What?" Jackson said. "Speak up, Canada."

"I said that's not fair," Isaac repeated, speaking much louder this time.

He stared at Jackson, clenching his teeth so hard that his jaw hurt. He realized he was struggling not to cry.

"Too bad," Jackson said. "My beach, my rules." He reached out with both hands and shoved Isaac's shoulders.

Isaac wasn't ready for it, and he fell backward, dropping his board and landing on his back in the sand. His elbow landed on a ragged rock.

Jackson's friends cracked up. With one last look at Isaac, the crew of local boys grabbed their boards and headed for the water.

Isaac sat there for only a moment. Then he grabbed his stuff and walked home as fast as he could, his surfboard under his arms.

CHAPTER 7

THROWING IN THE TOWEL

Isaac's mom was outside when he got home. She stood next to the family car with a soggy and soapy giant sponge. The car was covered with suds and water.

"Hey, Isaac," she said as he got closer to the house. "What happened to your arm?"

Isaac tried to look at his arm, but it was impossible to do while he held his surfboard.

"I guess I scraped it," he muttered.

Mom dropped her sponge into the big bucket next to the car and stooped at Isaac's side. She took the surfboard out of his hands and leaned it against the stoop.

"Did this happen while you were surfing?" she asked, inspecting his arm.

"I guess," Isaac said. "I must have scraped my arm on a rock underwater or something."

"You didn't feel it?" Mom asked. "It looks like it hurt." She stood up and put her hands on her hips. "Come inside. Let's get it cleaned up and find a bandage."

* * *

Fifteen minutes later, Isaac sat at the dining room table with his mom. He had a fresh bandage on his arm. A plate of cookies sat in front of them.

"So do you want to talk about what really happened?" Mom asked. She nibbled her cookie and looked Isaac right in the eye.

"What do you mean?" Isaac asked. He looked down to avoid his mom's gaze.

Mom leaned back in her chair and crossed her arms. Her shirt was still damp from washing the car.

"I mean you were only gone for fifteen minutes," she said. "Why'd you come home so quick?"

Isaac shrugged and wiped his mouth with the back of his hand. "I'm all done," he said, hopping up from his chair.

Mom grabbed his wrist. "Hold on a minute," she said. "Tell me."

"It was just some kids at the beach," Isaac said. "It's not a big deal."

"What did they do?" Mom asked.

"Nothing," Isaac said. "They're just not very nice. One of them shoved me."

"And that's nothing?" Mom asked. "Is that how you hurt your arm?"

"I guess," Isaac said, shrugging. He explained how he'd met Jackson his first day in town, and how Jackson had claimed the whole coast as his own. "Can I go now?"

Mom sighed. "Yes," she said. "But do you know any of these kids' names?"

"Mom," Isaac said, "please don't do anything. It's not a big deal."

"He hurt you!" she said.

"I can handle it," Isaac insisted. "I'll toughen up."

Mom reached out and grabbed Isaac's hand. "Honey, it's not an issue of you toughening up," she said. "This boy is going to keep doing this. You won't be able to surf anymore."

Isaac pulled his hand away and headed toward his bedroom. "Who cares," he muttered. "I don't like it anyway."

CHAPTER 8

DOOMED

Isaac lay on his bed after dinner. It had been a quiet meal. Dad asked about what happened at the beach earlier, and Isaac repeated the story as quickly and briefly as he could. After that, no one really said much.

As he flipped through his comic book, there was a knock at his bedroom door.

"Come in," he called, and Dad stuck his head through the open door.

"Hey, bud," Dad said as he sat on the bed next to Isaac. Isaac closed his comic book and sat up.

"I wanted to talk to you about this bully at the beach," Dad went on.

"Can't we just forget about it?" Isaac said, sitting up and rolling his eyes.

"That's the last thing we should do," Dad said. "Bullying isn't okay. If we forget about it, then the bully gets a free pass."

Isaac stared across the room at the bare walls. He hadn't even put up his snowboarding posters yet.

"Now, what's his name?" Dad asked.

Isaac sighed. He knew his dad wasn't going to give up. "It's Jackson," he said. "I don't know his last name. Actually, that might be his last name."

Dad nodded slowly. "Well, I'll have to look into this," he said. "And I'll be speaking to his parents."

"Dad, don't!" Isaac said. "He'll think I'm just some whiny baby."

"I'm sorry, Isaac," Dad said as he got to his feet. "I know it feels unfair to you right now, but this boy needs to know that what he's done is unacceptable."

As Isaac stood up, Dad left the room and closed the door behind him. Isaac let himself fall backward onto the bed.

Great, he thought. *I'm doomed.*

CHAPTER 9

HANGING TEN

Dad made good on his promise to find out who Jackson was. He made some phone calls, took a walk around the neighborhood and the beach, and eventually found Jackson's parents. He told them what had happened.

Isaac didn't hear the conversation, but he didn't have to. He was mortified. There was no way he could go back to the beach now.

That's the end of me surfing, Isaac thought.

Weeks passed, and Isaac continued avoiding the beach. Now he wasn't just scared of Jackson. He was also too embarrassed to show his face there.

Since surfing was out, Isaac spent most of his time at the comic book shop on the main street. He managed to make a few friends there.

One day toward the end of the summer, Isaac and one of his new friends, Ben, headed to Isaac's house for lunch after a trip to the comic shop.

After they ate, the boys headed to Isaac's room to read their comics. Isaac's surfboard, which hadn't been in the water in weeks, still leaned against his bedroom wall.

"Cool!" Ben said. "I didn't know you surfed."

Isaac shook his head. "I don't," he said. "Not anymore. I tried once or twice and totally failed."

"Once or twice?" Ben said. He ran a hand over the board. "And you just gave up? That's pretty dumb. It takes a long time to really learn how to surf."

Isaac shrugged. "Yeah, I guess it is," he admitted. "The truth is, there's this guy down there I'm avoiding. His name is Jackson."

"Yeah," Ben said. "He's a real jerk."

"You know him?" Isaac said.

"Sure," said Ben. "You're going to see him plenty once school starts next week. He's in our grade."

Isaac hadn't thought about that. If he was going to have to see Jackson at school all the time, avoiding the beach didn't make much sense.

And I really do want to learn to surf, Isaac thought.

He stood up from his desk and grabbed his board. "Come on," he said to Ben. "We're going to the beach."

* * *

"Aren't you worried about Jackson?" Ben asked as they walked up the boardwalk toward the beach.

"I am," Isaac admitted. "But I'd better get used to it if he's probably going to be in my class anyway."

"Or you could switch classes to avoid him all year," Ben said with a grin.

"That sounds a little too complicated," Isaac said.

When they reached the beach, Isaac scanned the crew of surfers in the water. It was crowded. It seemed like the entire neighborhood was out to catch a few waves before school started.

"There he is," Ben said, pointing at the water.

Jackson was under a huge cresting wave, about to be swallowed up by the barrel. The two boys watched as Jackson finished his run and surfed into the beach like a pro. He hopped off his board, picked it up, and immediately spotted Isaac.

"Uh-oh," Ben said. "He sees you."

Jackson handed his board to a friend and walked toward Isaac.

"Oh, man," Ben whispered, sounding nervous. "Here it comes."

Jackson's jaw was clenched as he stepped right up to Isaac and Ben. Isaac narrowed his eyes, not sure what to expect. He didn't know if Jackson was going to shove him or hit him or tell him off.

But Jackson didn't do any of those things. Instead, he took a deep breath and held out his hand.

Isaac just stared at it a moment, unsure what to do. Then he reached out and shook Jackson's hand.

Jackson let go of Isaac's hand, nodded once, and went back to get his surfboard. A moment later, he was out on the water again, paddling out to catch another big wave.

"Uh, what was that all about?" Ben asked, looking confused.

"I think that's the end of it," Isaac said.

Ben stared at him. "What are you, a ninja or something?" he asked.

Isaac laughed. He had a feeling it was his dad's talk with Jackson's parents that had really made the difference.

"Come on," Isaac said. "Let's try this surfing thing one more time."

With that, the two boys headed for the water and joined the rest of the surfers, taking turns on Isaac's board until the sun came down over the water.

AUTHOR BIO

Eric Stevens lives in St. Paul, Minnesota. He is studying to become a middle-school English teacher. Some of his favorite things include pizza, playing video games, watching cooking shows on TV, riding his bike, and trying new restaurants. Some of his least favorite things include olives and shoveling snow.

ILLUSTRATOR BIO

Aburtov has worked in the comic book industry for more than 11 years. In that time, he has illustrated popular characters like Wolverine, Iron Man, Blade, and the Punisher. He lives in Monterrey, Mexico, with his daughter, Ilka, and his beloved wife.

GLOSSARY

accent (AK-sent) — the way you pronouce words

access (AK-sess) — a way to enter or an approach to a place

complicated (KOM-pli-kay-tid) — something that is difficult to understand

cresting (KREST-ing) — reaching the highest point

dismal (DIZ-muhl) — gloomy and sad

dune (DOON) — a sand hill made by the wind near the ocean or a large lake or in a desert

nervous (NUR-vuhss) — fearful or timid

shallow (SHAL-oh) — not deep

unacceptable (uhn-uhk-SEP-tuh-buhl) — not good enough to be allowed or accepted

DISCUSSION QUESTIONS

1. Isaac doesn't want to tell his parents about the bully at the beach. Do you think he made the right decision? Talk about why or why not.

2. If you had a choice, would you rather surf or snowboard? Talk about your choice.

3. Why do you think Jackson was so mad that Isaac wanted to learn to surf? Talk about some possible reasons.

WRITING PROMPTS

1. Isaac isn't excited to move from the mountains to the beach. Have you ever had to move? Write a paragraph about how you dealt with it.

2. How would you feel if you were Isaac's parents? Write about what you would have done if you were in their shoes.

3. Write a paragraph about some other ways Issac could have handled the problems he was having with Jackson.

QUICK FACTS ABOUT SURFING

- Some surfers want to ride very tall waves. They have jet skis or boats to pull them far out into the ocean. Then they ride the waves all the way back to the beach.

- Some surfers like to windsurf. They use a special kind of surfboard with a sail attached to it. Wind catches the sail and pushes the surfer forward.

- White water that gently flows onto the beach is referred to as "soup" by many surfers.

- Some of the tallest waves in the world are found off the islands of Hawaii.

- Hawaiians invented both surfing and bodyboarding.

- There are three different types of surfboards: minimals, short boards, and long boards.

- Minimals are good surfboards for beginners. Long boards and short boards are for more advanced surfers.

MORE SURFING TERMINOLOGY:

- Catch a wave — to start a ride
- Hang ten — hanging all ten toes over the nose of a surfboard
- Ride the tube — to surf the space underneath a curling wave
- Wipeout — falling completely off the board